I0574768

OVER THE FALLS
WITH
GABBY AND MADDOX

OVER THE FALLS

WITH GABBY AND MADDOX

Steve Altier

The Little Horsemen™

The Little Horsemen Publications
A division of 4 Horsemen Publications, Inc.
1497 Main St. Suite 169
Dunedin, FL 34698
4horsemenpublications.com
info@4horsemenpublications.com

Sketches by Victoria Deutsch
Art Coloring by Vanity Diaz
Cover Typography and Typesetting by Autumn Skye
Edited by Gayle Staggemeyer

Library of Congress Control Number: 2023934411

Paperback ISBN-13: 978-1-64450-922-7
Hardcover ISBN-13: 978-1-64450-923-4
Audiobook ISBN-13: 978-1-64450-925-8
Ebook ISBN-13: 978-1-64450-924-1

DEDICATION.

Thank you to Victoria Deutsch for
your outstanding sketches.

Table of Contents

one

Hide-and-Seek

"**E**ight, nine, ten… here I come!" Maddox spun from the corner and began his search for his nine-year-old sister Gabby. "Where could she be hiding?" Maddox whispered to himself as he opened his bedroom door and glanced from side to side. *She wouldn't dare come into my room; the sign on the door clearly said, "No Girls Allowed…except for Mom."* Maddox pivoted on his heels and journeyed down the hallway that was lined with family photos that Mother had taken.

Slowly, he made his way to Gabby's room. Extending his hand, he wrapped his fingers firmly around the doorknob and twisted. The door swung wide, and he glanced left, then right, and tip-toed toward the pink blanket and pile of pillows that lined her bed. Slowly, he lifted the side of the bedspread and stared at the space under the bed. *That would have been too easy.*

He glared toward her closet, even though he knew how much junk she stored inside and didn't think there would be enough space for her to hide. But still, it was worth the look. He pulled the folding doors wide, and just as he suspected, there was nothing but girly clothes and piles of boxes.

He turned his attention to the hallway closet, which he knew was packed with blankets, towels, and sheets. But there was enough room to hide under the bottom shelf— something he knew from experience—but would Gabby use one of his hiding spots? He paused in front of the door. "I know you're in there," he said, then quickly thrust the door open. He frowned at another dead end.

She wouldn't dare hide in Mom and Dad's bedroom. The thought churned in his mind. Knowing Gabby the way he did, oh yeah, she was brave enough to hide in the only room they were told never to play in. He inched his way closer to their door. Bit by bit, he reached for the handle before pulling his hand back. His heart pounded. *I can do this; she's not going to win this time.* Butterflies filled his stomach, and his breathing grew louder as he laid his fingers on the doorknob. *Be brave; don't let her win.* He turned the knob until he heard the *click*, and the door inched open.

He peered through the thin crack, and with his foot, he bumped it open wider to get a better look. He gazed over his shoulder, trying to get a read on Mother's location. Was she still in the kitchen making dinner? He knew what he was about to do was wrong, but he ducked into his parents' bedroom and pushed the door closed with his rump. Extending his arm to his face, he wiped a bead of sweat from his forehead. *I have to be quick, like a ninja.* Taking a few steps forward, he quickly glanced under the bed. Just a few storage boxes Mother kept out of sight.

He darted toward the closet and opened the large doors, finding clothes, shoes, and some of Mother's fancy hats, but no Gabby. He darted to the master bathroom and looked in the shower and tub, but nothing was there. *Dang, Gabby is good at hiding.*

Maddox made his way back to the door, and just as he was about to open it and slide out, he heard footsteps on the stairs. Panic set in, and his palms began to sweat. It had to be Mother, and he would likely be busted—and grounded for playing in their bedroom. He darted toward the bed and quickly slid under; his nerves rattled as he lay trembling under the bed.

The door creaked open as Mother entered, humming a little tune. She emptied the clothes basket on the bed and began folding and hanging clothes. Maddox lay as still as he could and tried to control his breathing. Getting caught was the last thing he needed.

Mother darted back and forth, like a bee in the garden going from flower to flower. She flitted from the closet to the dresser as she folded and hung clothes. *Please hurry.* Maddox's heart raced. He didn't know how long he could hold out. Sweat beaded on his forehead, and he wouldn't put it past Gabby to come looking for him just to get him in trouble. His heart pounded harder as he watched his mother's feet pace back and forth.

Finally, she made her way to the door, opened it, then closed it behind her. A calm rush flooded over Maddox as he heard the soft *click* of the door. Seconds, maybe minutes, passed, and he slowly crawled from under the bed and lunged for the door. His breathing increased as he turned the knob and inched the door open a sliver.

Maddox's heart stopped when he spotted Mother standing at the top of the stairs with her arms folded over her chest. "Why were you in my room?"

Maddox froze, his face half-hidden behind the door. "Ah… um, I-I was, ah… looking for Gabby?"

"And what makes you think she would be in my room?"

"Ah, we were playing a game of hide-and-seek." Maddox twitched and scuffed his foot back and forth on the carpet, waiting for Mother to blow up.

"Well, I don't think you will find her in my room." She turned and made her way down the stairs.

That was it? No punishment? He broke a rule, and Mother didn't like rule-breakers. The toilet flushed in the hall bathroom, and Gabby strolled out, smiling. "Did you really think I would hide in Mom and Dad's bedroom?" She smirked and beamed with pride. Yet, she wondered why Maddox wasn't grounded.

Flabbergasted, he shook his head. *Why didn't I look in the hall bathroom first?* Before Maddox could respond, the front door opened, and Father's famous words echoed throughout the house. "I'm home!"

Maddox snapped out of his stupor and dashed for the stairs. Gabby was a few steps ahead of him and skipped every other step as she made her way down the stairs. She dashed to her father and wrapped her arms around his waist. Maddox tried to replicate his sister's fancy footwork, but his short legs from being two years younger hampered his efforts. Finally clearing the bottom step, he threw his arms around Father and embraced him.

"Dad! Dad, I got an A in math today," he bellowed, pulling a wrinkled piece of paper from his pocket and shoving it in front of his father's face. Father smiled and gathered Maddox up into his arms.

"That's great, buddy. I told you, hard work pays off." Father beamed.

"I know! My teacher was so impressed. She placed a gold star on the top."

"I see that." His grin grew wide.

Gabby held tight to her father's leg as he carried Maddox and Gabby to the kitchen. "Something smells good in here," he said as he lowered Maddox to the ground.

Mother spun around. "Oh, I didn't hear you come in." She smiled, extending her arms for a hug as Father embraced her.

"What smells so good?" he whispered.

"I'm making my grandma's old recipe, chicken and dumplings."

"Oh, I love it." He gave Mother a soft kiss on the cheek. "I better get changed; Maddox has baseball practice tonight, and I don't want to be late." Father patted Maddox on the butt. "Why don't you get changed and grab your baseball gear, so the minute we are done eating, we can go? Wanna race?"

Maddox dashed to the stairs, with Father one step behind, and the laughter faded as the two pounded up the stairs.

Gabby gazed at the stairs, wishing she could play baseball like the boys. She was good with the glove and not bad at batting, either. But Mother had enrolled her in dance, and she didn't want to disappoint her mother—after all, it seemed to make her happy.

"Gabby, can you set the table please?"

"Sure, Mom." Gabby frowned as she thought about swinging the bat and making contact with the ball like she had a few times during recess. She wrapped her tiny fingers around a stack of plates and set them on the table. Then, she pulled the drawer open, counted four knives, forks, and spoons, and laid them on the table. She grabbed the glasses Mother had set on the counter and placed them onto the table. Mother always helped with the glasses since Gabby was not tall enough to reach the upper cabinets. Gabby proceeded to arrange the place settings in order: plate in the center, napkin to the left, silverware to the right, and glass in front of the plate.

"That looks great, dear. Can you grab a few pot-holders for me?"

Gabby opened a lower drawer and snatched three cloth potholders and placed them in the center of the table. She watched Mother set a large pot of chicken and dumplings on one, a pot of mashed potatoes on another, and the dinner roll basket on the last.

Thundering footsteps echoed from the living room as the boys dashed in and took their seats.

"Did you wash your hands?"

"We sure did," Maddox blurted out. Father nodded in approval as he slid the chair out for Mother to take her seat.

"Thank you, dear."

Father grabbed the large spoon and dished up Gabby's plate, then Maddox's, as Mother took care of herself. Finally, he piled a large amount of chicken, dumplings, and potatoes on his plate, and they began to dig in.

"So, Gabby, how was your day at school?" Father asked.

"Oh, you know, nothing special, just a little bit of home-work." She squirmed a little in her seat.

Mother noticed and wondered what Gabby was hiding but decided not to pry in front of the boys.

Dinner was over in a flash, and Father and Maddox sprinted to the door and let it slam behind them as they headed to baseball practice. "I wish I could go," Gabby grumbled under her breath.

"Maybe we can watch next time, dear. Now, will you please help me clean up the table?" Mother turned and started to pack up the leftovers and piled the dishes into the dishwasher.

Gabby frowned as she handed Mother one plate at a time. *I don't want to watch; I want to play.* She handed Mother one of the pots and then another. Soon the table was clear, and Mother tossed her a wet towel, which Gabby swished back and forth on the table until every last inch was clean.

Gabby grabbed her backpack and pulled out a tablet and a book, tossing them onto the table. She looked at the math problems on the page and dreamed she could hear the crack of the bat as she scooped up the ground ball and tossed it to first base for the out.

Mother gazed at Gabby. "That homework is not going to finish itself."

"Sorry, Mom." Gabby stared at the page.

Mother turned her attention to the television, and Gabby focused on her homework before joining her mother. "When your father gets home, we have some exciting news to share with you both." Mother smiled.

Gabby perked up. "Mom, please tell me. I promise not to say a word. Please!"

"I promised your father we would tell you both at the same time."

"But I'm the oldest; I should know first."

"I'm sorry, honey, but I gave my word." Mother paused as a smile spread across her face. "Vacation."

"What? Vacation?"

"That's all I can say."

Gabby's mind raced. They had already been to Italy, so where were they off to this time? *Paris? London? Oh, maybe Sweden or Germany!* The possibilities were endless. Gabby couldn't wait to tell Maddox she knew a secret.

Time slowed as Gabby waited for Maddox to get home. Her mind wandered as she thought about how she was going to play this. Just a slight hint that she knew something he didn't? Or should she drop the bomb and say, "We're going on a vacation, and I'm not telling you where?"

Gabby turned her attention to the driveway as a car rolled to a screeching halt. Her heart quickened; the time had come. She decided to go with option one and let Maddox know she knew a secret, just to keep him on edge.

The car door slammed, and the front door swung open. Gabby was ready to pounce as Maddox came skipping in, and before Mother could ask how practice was, he blurted at the top of his lungs, "We're going to Niagara Falls! We're going to Niagara Falls!" Maddox shot Gabby a wry smile and proceeded up the stairs to his bedroom. "We're going to Niagara Falls!"

"Mom!" Gabby screamed as a tear traced down the side of her cheek.

Mother crossed her arms and stared at Father as he entered the house. He stopped and lowered his head. "Sorry. He had a great practice, and he wanted to stop for ice cream; so instead, I told him we were planning a vacation to Niagara Falls."

Gabby sobbed and darted past her father and stomped up the stairs. Mother stood fast and gazed at Father. The sound of a door slamming echoed down the hallway, letting everyone know Gabby was upset.

"You gave me your word."

Father bowed his head. "It's just a vacation…"

"Just a vacation?" Mother gave him a sidelong stare. "You gave your word."

"I guess I should talk to Gabby, huh?"

"Yeah, I think you should."

TWO

The Ballgame

Father turned and proceeded to the stairs, but he paused and looked over his shoulder. Mother pointed upward, and he swallowed hard and journeyed forward. "Knock, knock," Father said in a soft tone.

"Go away," Gabby sobbed.

"Hey, honey, I didn't mean to ruin the surprise." He paused. "You should be happy that we are planning another vacation. I know how much you enjoy traveling and learning about new places." Father leaned forward, placing his ear against the door. All was quiet on the inside, giving him a warm feeling that Gabby was going to be fine. "I'm sorry, I truly am. Anyway, Mother asked me to tell you that we are going to have some ice cream… It's your favorite, choco-late. I hope you will join us." Father turned and took a few steps toward the stairs.

"I'll race you," Maddox shouted as he dashed past, wearing his bright red pajamas.

"Not tonight, sport." Father frowned and gazed back at Gabby's door before he proceeded down the stairs to the dining room. He pulled out Mother's chair for her so she could sit, then took his own.

"I take it Gabby's not going to join us?"

"It doesn't look that way."

A creaking sound echoed from the stairwell, putting smiles on both Mother and Father's faces. Slowly, Gabby peeked her head around the corner and surveyed the situation. Maddox shot her a smug look as he shoveled a large spoonful of ice cream into his mouth.

"Don't look at your sister like that," Mother said, her tone sharp. His smile quickly vanished.

Gabby slowly walked over and took her seat as her mother slid a bowl of chocolate ice cream in front of her.

"How was practice?" Mother asked.

"I only missed two balls that were hit in my direction and struck out once in batting practice." Maddox swayed back and forth in his chair with pride. "Can you tell us more about our trip?"

Gabby looked up but tried to hide her interest. "Well, it's one of the largest waterfalls in the world. And we plan to take a helicopter ride over the falls and a boat ride to the base of the falls." Mother smiled.

"I can't wait." Maddox bounced in his seat.

Gabby remained silent, focusing on the ice cream in front of her, though it wasn't long before the ice cream was gone. Maddox and Father bounced up and began clearing the table and washing the dishes. Father had a rule: if you prepare the meal, you don't have to clean up. Father was all about teamwork, except when Maddox was late for ball practice. It didn't take long, and the dishes were cleaned and back on the shelves where they belonged. Father and Maddox joined the ladies to watch a little TV before going to bed.

Saturday came quickly. Maddox had an early baseball game, and the entire family gathered to watch. Gabby sat in the bleachers with envy. She knew she could hit and catch better than most of the boys on the team. It wasn't fair that she couldn't play. It didn't make sense. The questions boiled inside. Was it her mother's rule? Was it because she felt Gabby should dance? Or was it a baseball rule? She was going to have to do a little research.

Gabby watched as Maddox walked to the on-deck circle. He bent over, picked up his bat, and began swinging the bat back and forth. The crowd cheered at the crack of the bat. Gabby's eyes darted to the batter at the plate. She caught a glimpse of the baseball soaring over the second base-man's head and landing in centerfield. The runner stopped at first base.

"Come on, Maddox, drive him home," Gabby yelled. Father smiled at her with pride before turning his attention to home plate, where Maddox stood waiting for the pitcher to throw the ball.

The pitcher took his position and pulled the ball back behind his head, then thrust his arm forward and burned the ball past Maddox, who watched the ball land in the catcher's glove.

"Strike one," the umpire hollered.

"Come on, Maddox, swing the bat," Father wailed.

The pitcher wound up the pitch and let it fly. "Strike two," the umpire cried out.

Maddox stood poised in the batter's box. He swung the bat a time or two and bent his knees, staring at the pitcher. The young man wound his arm behind his head and, in one quick motion, let the ball soar at Maddox, who ducked and hit the ground in time to avoid being hit by the ball.

"Ball," the umpire yelled and reached to help Maddox to his feet.

Maddox stood outside the batter's box and dusted him-self off. He placed one foot inside the batter's box, then slowly placed the second foot in and took one practice swing before assuming his position. Maddox nodded at the pitcher to let him know he was ready.

The pitcher coiled up and brought his arm forward, sending a searing pitch toward home plate. Maddox gazed at the ball and brought his bat forward with all his might, spinning the bat past the ball. "Strike three!"

"Dang it," Maddox yelled and lightly tossed the bat toward the on-deck circle.

Gabby sprung to her feet and ran to the wire fence that separated the fans from the players. "Plant your back foot and keep your eyes on the ball. Don't swing so hard; you just need to make contact. I know you can do this." Gabby smiled at her little brother.

Maddox stepped up to the plate two innings later. The pitcher wound up and let the ball fly toward home plate. Maddox planted his back foot, eyes fixed on the ball, and brought the bat forward in one easy motion. A loud *pop* rang out as Maddox struck the ball with the fat part of the bat. The crowd went wild, and Maddox darted toward first base. Maddox noticed his coach yelling to keep running, and Maddox touched first base and poured on the speed as he made his way to second base. The third base coach was waving his arms in a circular motion, and Maddox glanced to the outfield to see where the ball was as he touched second base and plowed his way toward third.

"Slide," the coach cheered. "Slide!"

Maddox hesitated, unsure if he should slide in feet-first or head-first. In a split second, he chose to be dramatic and dove headfirst at third base, going right under the third basemen's glove as he caught the ball.

"Safe." The third base umpire extended his arms to the sides to let the crowd know the runner made it to the plate before the ball arrived. Mother, Father, and Gabby bounced to their feet and cheered Maddox on.

Maddox watched as the next batter stepped to the plate. "Please hit the ball," Maddox whispered. The pitcher wound up and threw the ball. The batter swung and hit the ball over the first basemen's head. Maddox threw his arms in the air and trotted to home plate and, with both feet, jumped onto the bag to score his first run of the season. His teammates lined up to slap his hand as he ran past and made his way to the dugout. Maddox paused and tilted his ball cap to Gabby. He mouthed the words, "thank you" and smiled as he went inside to join his companions.

The game lasted a little over an hour, and Maddox's team lost six to one. But still, this was a call to celebrate, as Maddox knew the one on the scoreboard belonged to him.

Three

The Adventure Begins

The final two weeks of school had come to a close. Gabby was thrilled to be moving on to the fifth grade, and Maddox was moving up to third. Summer vacation was upon them, and for Gabby and Maddox, that meant another adventure. For the past two weeks, they had been on the Internet doing a little research about the falls. They wanted to check out the large rapids and the Cave of Winds at the base of the falls.

The big day had finally arrived, and Maddox hustled about, stuffing clothes into his duffle bag before finally zipping it up. Maddox tossed his bag over his shoulder while Gabby pushed her extra-large pink suitcase toward the stairs.

"Why did you pack so much?" Maddox bounced on the balls of his feet, pausing to watch his sister struggle with her bag.

"You know, Mom said people die at Niagara Falls," Gabby blurted out with a sharp tone in her voice.

"What does that have to do with you packing so much? And just so you know, I'm not scared. Dad said people die when they do stupid things, like trying to go over the falls in a barrel." Maddox glared at his sister.

"I'm telling Mom you called me stupid."

"I did not!" Maddox couldn't believe his ears. "Why would you say that?"

"Okay, I'll tell you what; I won't tell Mom if you carry my bag to the car."

"Alright, I'll carry your bag, but you still never answered my question." Maddox snatched the handle and slowly dragged, pushed, and pulled the pink suitcase down the stairs and out the door. He placed it near the rear of the car.

"Oh, honey, that was so sweet of you." Mother beamed with delight.

"Anything for my sister." Maddox smiled, seizing the moment.

Father gave Maddox a slight nod and smile as he packed the final bags into the car. "It looks like we're ready to hit the road."

Mother and Gabby were the last two in the car. Mother took the seat next to Father, and Gabby sat in the rear next to her brother. Maddox looked on and watched as Gabby slid her headphones over her ears, turned on her tablet, and began watching a movie.

The car backed out of the driveway and pulled forward, leaving their house in small-town Ohio and heading east toward Pennsylvania.

Just like that, their adventure had begun.

"Mom, Mom!"

Mother turned to look at Gabby. "Yes, dear?"

"I think I forgot something."

"What would that be?"

"I'm not sure… I may have left a light on. Or forgot to feed Boots and Momma. Who's taking care of them, anyway?"

"Gabby, I double-checked all the lights; they were off. Boots and Momma have plenty of food and litter boxes. Plus, my friend Cindy is going to check on them daily."

"Are you sure I didn't forget something?"

"I'm pretty sure." Mother nodded as she turned to face the front. "Besides, if you forgot something, there are plenty of stores where we can shop."

The hours passed. Father stopped once for a bathroom break and once for lunch. By late afternoon, the family had traveled hundreds of miles and were making their way to Amish country, deep in the heart of Lancaster, Pennsylvania. Mother began to explain that the Amish lived off the land and didn't use electricity or drive cars. Father slowed as they drove past a farm, where they saw a man dressed in black and white, riding on a plow behind a few horses as the dust flew in the air.

"Wow, that looks like hard work," Maddox blurted out. "It must take them all day."

"I'm sure it does," Gabby snarled.

Father slowed, then pulled into the left lane, passing a horse and black buggy. Maddox sprang up, turned around, and stared as they passed. He noticed a man wearing black pants and a long-sleeved black shirt with a nice cream-colored hat and a long, black beard. He pulled on the ropes that were attached to the bridle on the horses trotting in front of the black-covered buggy. Next to him sat a woman wearing a black dress and a scarf over her hair. Maddox noticed two young kids behind them in the back, a boy and a girl wearing clothes that matched their parents.

"They're a family, just like us," Maddox whispered to himself. He extended his hand and waved. "The Amish look cool."

"The Amish share traditional Christian beliefs, but they are farmers of all kinds. Farming has been the center of Amish work life. However, I read that in the past century, an increasing number of Amish people are becoming involved in business enterprises, most notably in carpentry and sales of farm products. I also hear they make awesome baked goods," Mother added.

"That's pretty cool. Do they have computers?" Gabby asked.

"I don't think so, since they don't have electricity. But I'm not one hundred percent sure," Mother said.

"Could we be Amish?" Maddox asked, and Gabby laughed while Mother chuckled.

"I don't think so, dear," Mother added. "Did you know there are also Mennonites?"

"What's a Mennonite?" Gabby asked.

"Well, from what I understand, the Amish live in close-knit communities and don't become part of the main population like where we live. However, Mennonites can live as part of the population, and they are not as strict as the Amish. So, a Mennonite family could have electricity and a computer. But keep in mind, I'm not an expert on the subject," Mother said.

"Well then, I want to be a Mennonite," Maddox chimed in, and the family could not contain their laughter over Maddox's excitement.

The day was winding down, leaving only an hour before nightfall. Mother and Father decided to get a room for the night when they spotted a cute little family motel along the road. Adjacent to the motel was a small family diner that served family-style dinners. Mother and Father were thrilled to be out of the car and resting for the evening, especially after being seated all day.

The waitress took everyone's order and headed to the kitchen. "What time will we arrive tomorrow?" Maddox asked.

"That depends on traffic and what time we get up," Father said.

"Does that mean early afternoon and late in the day?" Maddox asked again.

"We get there when we get there." Father chuckled and gave Maddox a look.

"I see." Maddox smiled back at Father as the waitress placed their dinner in front of them.

Gabby and Maddox dove into the food like they hadn't eaten for days. After dinner, Father stepped over to pay the bill, as Mother spotted Dutch whoopie pies and tossed a few of the cakes onto the counter. Gabby and Maddox's eyes bulged when they noticed the large, chocolate, cake-like cookies overflowing with white icing in the middle.

"These are Amish baked goods. We can have them when we get back to the room," Mother said with a grin.

"We had better get a half-gallon of milk to go with them," Father said as he grabbed the milk container from the small cooler next to the counter.

Gabby and Maddox walked slowly back to the room. "I can't wait to sink my teeth into one of those whoopie pies," Maddox whispered.

"Is that all you think about, food?" Gabby stared at her brother.

"No…" He paused. "I was thinking about seeing the falls tomorrow." Maddox glowed with excitement.

"Me, too." Gabby smiled and paused. "Hey, can you keep a secret?" Gabby gazed at her brother.

"Sure," he replied with confidence.

"Well," Gabby twitched as they stopped short of the door to their room. "I'm wondering if I should ask Mom if I can play baseball instead of going to dance class…"

"Yeah, why not? I know you would be great at baseball. I've seen you throw and hit at school, so it makes no sense why you shouldn't play." Maddox patted his sister on the back. "Just ask her; I know it will be fine."

"I don't want Mom getting mad." Gabby bounced on the balls of her feet.

"Mom's not going to get mad; she may be a little disappointed, but she will understand." Maddox rested his hand on her shoulder. "Dad is always saying to do what makes you happy, and this would make you happy."

"I don't know… I don't want to hurt Mom." Gabby frowned, not sure what to do about the dilemma she faced. *Should I hurt Mom's feelings, or should I do what makes her happy?* "I'll think about it for a while."

"Don't worry, I'll tell her for you."

"No!" Gabby grabbed Maddox's arm and pulled him close. "You keep your mouth shut. You promised!"

"Hey, that hurts. Let go of my arm."

"Is everything okay?" Father asked.

"Yes." Gabby released her brother's arm and strutted through the doorway.

Father looked Maddox over. "Everything okay, bud?"

"Yeah, everything is great." Maddox puffed out his chest and followed Gabby into the room.

"Strange kids," Father whispered to himself as he closed the door for the night.

Four

One More Day

Morning came quickly, and Gabby and Maddox scurried about the hotel room like a couple of mice trying to find some cheese. They took turns getting a shower and brushing their teeth as Mother laid out their clothes for the day and then packed her bag. The kids were ready in a flash and quickly stuffed things back into their suitcases, not wanting to leave anything behind. Mother paused for a moment, watching her family get ready. You could feel the excitement in the air. A few more hours on the road, and they would arrive at Niagara Falls, New York.

The car was packed, and Father walked back to the office to return the keys and check out. Soon, the car lunged forward, and they were headed to New York. Gabby started watching a girly movie. "Can we watch something else?" Maddox asked.

"No, I like this movie."

"But I don't, and you already watched this!"

"That was yesterday, silly." Gabby gave Maddox a stare.

"Enough, Gabby. Let your brother pick the movie today."

"But Mom—"

"You heard me. Now let your brother pick the movie."

"Fine," she grumbled as she passed the control to her brother. *Why does he always get his way?*

Maddox gazed at Gabby, knowing it was her fault, and Gabby wrinkled her nose and frowned back at Maddox. They both folded their arms over their chests and began to pout. Mother's keen eye caught wind of what was happening. "The two of you can get happy in the same pants you got mad in, or I'll turn the movie off!" Mother blurted out. "Do you understand?"

"Yes, ma'am." Gabby sighed, her eyes darting out the window to avoid looking at her mother.

"Yes, Mom," Maddox added, frowning as he looked at the sadness in his mother's eyes.

Father kept driving, and from time to time, Maddox would notice Father gazing in the rearview mirror to check on them. They went up and down on the rolling hills of the old country highway. Maddox couldn't help but notice the long rows of corn and hayfields. Cow pastures, red, wooden barns, and silos dotted the landscape. The scene was breathtaking. As the hours passed, the scenery began to change. Maddox noticed more cars and trucks surrounding them, and the landscape was covered with large billboards and buildings.

"Welcome to the city of Buffalo, New York," Gabby whispered.

"It won't be long now," Father added. "Just a few more miles to the hotel and the falls."

"Are we going to see the falls today?" Maddox asked.

"Well, once we get checked in at the hotel, I guess we can walk over and get a glimpse of the falls before going to dinner… if your father is okay with that?" Mother said.

Father smiled. "Of course, we can go see, hear, and even feel the mist from the falls before we get something to eat."

"Yeah!" Gabby and Maddox replied in unison.

"Well, it's good to see you both smiling now." Father chuckled.

"What's that?" Maddox pointed out the front window.

"That, my boy, is the mist rising into the air," Father replied.

"Where's it coming from?" Gabby asked.

"*Duh*. It's coming from the falls, silly."

"Mom, he called me a name."

"Maddox, no name-calling."

 Maddox frowned. "Sorry Mom, sorry Gabby."

"It's alright." Gabby was quick to forgive. Mother gave Maddox a quick stare, and Maddox bowed his head.

"The size and the amount of water going over the falls creates the mist when it hits the bottom. Then the mist rises into the air, and that is what you are seeing now." Father was full of facts. He loved to read about history and places of travel, so he could answer any questions the kids may have.

Father hit the button on the door next to him, and all the car windows went down at the same time. "Do you hear that?" The faint sound of a thundering roar grew as they approached.

"How far away are we?" Maddox asked.

"I would think less than a mile," Father replied.

"I hear it, but I don't see anything," Gabby said as she gazed at the mist floating in the air.

The entrance of the hotel came into view as the car rolled to a stop. "The falls are a good walking distance in that direction." Father pointed across the parking lot. "Now, if you kids don't mind, how about grabbing your bags so we can go to our room and get this adventure started?"

"Yeah!" they cheered. The doors flung open, and Gabby and Maddox grabbed their bags, then followed Mother and

Father toward the entrance of the hotel. After a brief stop at the receptionists' counter, they were off to the elevator. Gabby darted forward and pushed the up button to call the elevator. "I love elevators," she added.

Maddox nodded and stepped in front of his sister, so he would be the first one inside. "What floor?" He was anxious for his father to respond so he could push the button before Gabby.

"The top floor."

Maddox quickly began to count the buttons: two, three, four, five, six. There was no seven. So, six had to be the top floor, and the light began to glow. "What?"

"Beatcha." Gabby beamed with pride, still holding her finger on the button on the other side of the door.

"Ah man, Dad!" Maddox whined.

"Be quicker next time, sport." The elevator lunged upward. Moments later, the door slid open, and the siblings raced down the hall.

"What's our room number, dear?"

"Six-ten," Father replied.

"Oh, they went in the wrong direction." Mother had an evil grin. "Let's beat the kids," she whispered. Mother and Father quickly darted down the hallway in the opposite direction and stopped at their room, six hundred ten.

Father waved the card in front of the door, and the light turned green. He pushed the door open. "After you, dear." He smiled and winked as she entered.

Gabby and Maddox slowly walked up with their bags in tow, glancing at Father.

"That's right, Mother and I beat you both." He smiled and chuckled, closing the door behind him as he entered the room.

"So, what's next?" Maddox asked.

"First, we need to unpack a little, use the restrooms, and freshen up. Then your father and I will look at what there is to do, and we will let you know." Gabby and Maddox darted about the room, unpacking a few clothes and placing some personal items in the bathroom.

One by one, they used the restroom, and when Maddox finished, he noticed Gabby staring out the window. Maddox stood next to her. "Great view, right?" Maddox pointed at the city skyline and the large river off in the distance.

Gabby didn't flinch.

"Hey, what are you thinking about?"

"Baseball…"

"What? Baseball? Oh, my goodness, Gabby, just ask Mom, will you?" Maddox threw his arms up in the air and pointed toward the river. "We're at Niagara Falls, and all you can think about is playing baseball?"

"Yes." She paused and turned to her brother. "It's easy for you; you're a boy. You can play and do whatever you want. But I'm expected to dance because I'm a girl, and I don't want to," she whispered.

"Please," Maddox pleaded. "Just ask Mom; she will understand." He frowned and shook his head slightly. "Listen, when we get back home, we can talk to Mom and Dad together. I promise I will help you. Now, can we enjoy Niagara Falls?" He placed his arm around his sister and pulled her in close as they both gazed out the window at the beauty of the river that stretched for miles. "Do you see where the mist is and the water disappears? That's the top of the falls." He pulled Gabby in closer.

"That's amazing. I didn't think the falls were that big," Gabby murmured, stunned.

The bathroom door swung open, and Father raised his finger to his lips to shush Mother before she could say a word. She stopped, stood by his side, and hugged him. "I think they can see the falls," he whispered into her ear.

"I wish I had my camera; I'd take a picture." Mother sighed.

"I overheard Gabby and Maddox talk about something, but we can discuss it later when we're alone. It's good; I promise," Father whispered in Mother's ear.

Mother smiled back and gave him a big hug.

Five

Walking the Wire

Mother and Father discussed where to go first, and they decided to take a stroll through the park and along the top of the falls. The roar of the falls could be heard in the distance. Mother pointed at the Niagara Falls Museum, and they decided they should learn a little about the history of the town and the falls before tomorrow's big adventure. Father purchased the tickets, and the children scurried inside.

Pictures lined the walls. Black-and-white photos of days gone by slowly turned to color images of the modern day. The winter scenes, where the falls were covered in ice and snow, were captivating. The night pictures were awesome with all the different colored lights that they used on the falls.

Maddox stopped and clutched his father's hand. He gazed at a plaque, and Gabby nudged Maddox to check out his find. "3,160 tons of water flow over Niagara Falls every second? Holy cow, how much is that?" She turned to her father.

"Keep reading."

"75,750 gallons of water per second flow over the American and Bridal Veil Falls, and 681,750 gallons of water per second flow over the Horseshoe Falls," Gabby finished and gazed at Maddox, her eyes wide and her mouth open.

"Are there three waterfalls?" Maddox asked.

"It sure looks that way." Father smiled.

"Are we going to see them all?" Maddox's heart skipped a beat.

"Yes, that is why we came." Mother tapped him on the back.

"I'm over the moon excited," Gabby blurted out as she bounced on her toes.

"Keep reading," Mother coaxed Gabby.

"The water falls at thirty-two feet per second, hitting the base of the falls with 280 tons of force at the American and Bridal Veil Falls, and 2,509 tons of force at the base of the Horseshoe Falls." She paused. "How much force is that?"

"Enough to crush us all." Father wiggled his fingers and shot them a crazed smile.

"Cool," Maddox whispered.

"Stop that." Mother frowned. "It also says that the falls are capable of producing over 4 million kilowatts of electricity, which is shared by the United States and Canada."

The family slowly moved along, and Maddox pointed to a picture with no water going over the falls.

Gabby stepped forward. "In 1969, an earthen dam was built across the head of the American Rapids, de-watering the American Falls. For six months, geologists and engineers studied the rock face and the effects of erosion." Gabby turned to Mother. "It doesn't give us the results?"

Mother was puzzled, like Gabby. "Well, I guess that will give us something to research when we get back to the hotel."

As they moved along, Gabby spotted a large picture of a man walking over the falls on a tightrope. "June 15, 2012. Nik Wallenda, 'The King of the Wire,' known for his high-wire performances, successfully walked directly over Niagara Falls. The feat was broadcast internationally. For the walk, he was required to wear a safety harness for the first time in his life… That is so cool."

Gabby noticed two large barrels about fifty feet apart and a large wire about a foot off the ground stretched between them. The sign on the wall read, "Can you walk the tightrope?" Gabby tugged on Mother's arm and darted toward the wire. Stepping up on the small, one-foot square platform, she braced herself and slowly slid her right foot on the wire. Stretching her arms to her sides for balance, Gabby moved her left foot in front of the right and wobbled a little before she gained her balance. Her heart began to race, and her knees wobbled. She was on the wire, just like Nik Wallenda. Gabby beamed as she moved her right foot and placed it on the wire. Only forty-seven feet to finish the walk. *I can do this*. She placed her left foot as the mist began to rise. The roar of the falls echoed off the walls, and Gabby realized she was no longer in the museum; she was over the falls. Her teeth chattered, and her body tensed up.

Gabby was confused; one minute she was in the museum, and now, she was on a tightrope over the falls. *How could this have happened?* She couldn't waste time thinking about that now; she had to focus, and she pushed the thought out of her head.

The wire became slippery, and Gabby turned to look back but realized she was too far from the platform to turn around. She was left with only one decision, and that was to complete her high-wire performance. She steadied herself and placed one foot in front of the other. The wind howled, and the wire wobbled. Her arms flailed at her sides, and she quickly regained her balance.

Sweat trickled down her forehead and dropped into her eye. Her vision blurred and burned from the salt of her skin. Gabby slowly brought her right hand upward and removed the drop from her eye, then she wiped her arm over her forehead to eliminate the remaining sweat. Easing her arm to her side for balance, she steadied herself. *Focus.* Gabby moved one foot forward, then the other. *I can do this!* She moved her foot again, and slowly, she moved over the wire. Her heart raced with fear and excitement as she continued her journey.

Maddox strolled along, gazing at the pictures that hung from the wall. One photo showed odd-shaped barrels with men and women dressed in strange-looking clothes. "Father, why do they dress like that?" Maddox pointed to the picture with a man wearing a top hat.

"Well, these pictures were taken a long time ago. Take this one." Father pointed to the large metal barrel and a man wearing what looked like a captain's hat and a black bowtie. "This picture was taken in the late 1800s." Father paused and leaned forward. "Ah, Joseph Avery." He stopped. "Oh my…" Father shuffled along to the next picture.

Maddox followed his father, pointing toward a woman in the picture. "Did she go over the falls?"

Father gazed at the woman standing next to the over-sized barrel. "October 24, 1901. On her sixty-third birthday, Annie Edson Taylor, an American school teacher, was the first person to survive a trip over Niagara Falls in a barrel. Wow!"

"What? A girl did it first?" Maddox's jaw dropped.

"Why does that surprise you? Girls can do anything boys can, sometimes better." Father reached and ruffled

ANNIE EDSON TAYLOR
HEROINE OF NIAGARA FALLS
OCT
1901

Maddox's hair. Maddox shot Father a sidelong smirk and pulled away.

As he moved, he noticed Gabby walking on a tightrope suspended about a foot off the floor. Maddox darted over and quickly poked his sister in the arm. "Gabby, you got to see this." He paused, waiting for his sister to open her eyes. Growing impatient, Maddox yelled, "Gabby, check this out!" Then, he nudged Gabby again.

The wind howled, the wire wobbled, and the mist engulfed her, making it hard to see anything in front of her. Her knees buckled, and she almost lost her balance. Seagulls squawked as they flew past her body, and panic set in. What if she fell? Would she land in the water? How cold would the water be? She knew it would sting at first. *Relax,* she told herself. *I can do this. Focus.*

She glided a few inches forward as a bird nipped her arm. A strong gust of wind forced Gabby to lose her balance, and her foot missed the wire, and she fell to the right side. Her arms whirled in the air as she hurtled toward the cold water below.

Maddox frowned as Gabby lost her balance and landed on the floor. "I'm sorry."

"You pushed me," Gabby yelled, but then she realized she was lying on the museum floor and smiled. *I must have been dreaming,* Gabby thought to herself. Relief flooded her body, and she let out a little laugh.

Laughter rang out from a little girl standing behind a book rack, her eyes fixed on Gabby.

"What are you looking at?" Gabby snipped.

"You're lying on the floor," she snickered and moved toward Gabby. "Hi, I'm Addie." She held out her hand and helped Gabby to her feet. "Is this your first trip to the falls, eh?"

Gabby made eye contact with Addie. "Yes, my brother and I are visiting from Ohio. Where are you from?"

"We're from Canada, eh. I'm here with my brothers, too."

Two boys, one slightly younger than Gabby and the other about Gabby's age, appeared from one of the aisles and walked toward Gabby. "Are you making new friends, sis?" The older boy smiled, gazing at Gabby. "Hi, I'm Knox, and this is my brother Zander." He pointed to the young, shy lad standing behind him.

"Hello, I'm Gabby." She smiled as she gently brushed her hair from her eyes.

"Are you alright?" Knox asked. "It looks like you fell."

Gabby blushed. "Yes, I lost my balance."

"Well, I'm impressed. You almost made it to the end; I would have fallen in the first two or three feet." He laughed.

"Um-hmm." Maddox coughed into his hand.

"Sorry, this is my brother Maddox," Gabby introduced him to her new friends. A painting on the wall caught his attention, and he started to read the story when Gabby interrupted and started reading out loud.

"The year was 1827, and a group of hotel owners thought the massive waterfall itself just wasn't enough. One of the hotel owners purchased a condemned boat and called it '*Pirate Michigan*.' Other business owners joined in and began advertising their scheme. The announcement was intriguing. The pirate ship *Michigan*, with a cargo of ferocious wild animals, will pass the great rapids and falls of Niagara on 8th September 1827, at six o'clock. They were said to be young and of superior musculature, so a great many were expected to survive the horrendous trip. The actual animals documented were a buffalo, two small bears, two raccoons, a dog, and a goose.

"On the appointed day, the animals were assembled, and visitors were allowed to board the boat and view them. A large crowd had gathered as the vessel was pointed to the falls and released; the ship bobbed up and down and rocked back and forth in the perilous waters. At the rapids, the hull was torn open, and the two bears escaped, swimming to Goat Island. But the others were tied or caged. Only a lone goose survived to the base of the falls. The stunt backfired, and the outcry by the people was heard. Many owners lost their businesses."

"That's horrible! They sent a dog over the falls and other animals," Gabby wept as tears traced down her cheeks.

"I'm sorry." Knox's voice was sincere. "I feel your pain; we have two dogs, and I would never hurt them or any other animal. That was disgusting," he added.

"Yeah… we have two cats, Boots and Momma." Gabby stuttered, trying to regain herself and appear strong.

"Momma?" Knox was puzzled.

"Yes, my dad found her at his job. She had two kittens, so he called her Momma, trying to gain her trust. He fed them daily, and time passed. Well, one day, Momma and Gray—we named him Gray—showed up to eat, but the other kitten was not with her. He never saw the second kitten after that day. Father decided to capture them and bring them home, and he did."

"I thought you said you only had two cats? Did you change the name to Boots?" Knox asked.

"No, poor Gray was sick, and after six months, he passed. It was a sad day for all of us, including Momma, because she had lost her son. But she is happy now and loves her family. We treat them both special because they are family to us." Gabby felt better after telling her story.

"I guess we can't save them all, but that was nice that your dad tried to."

The group chatted for a few minutes before Mother and Father told them it was time to go.

"Later, dudes." Maddox smiled as he gave Knox and Zander fist bumps.

"Will we see you again?" Gabby asked Knox, with a glance toward Addie and Zander.

"I sure hope so." Knox smiled.

"Bye." Gabby waved, turned, and hurried toward her family. She paused and looked back to see Knox gazing at her, too. She blushed.

"Gross!" Maddox snickered. "You like him."

"I do not!" Gabby rebelled.

"Come on, kiddos, we need to eat, get back to the hotel, and get a good night's sleep. We have a busy day tomorrow," Father stated.

cave of the winds

The sun beamed through the hotel curtains and danced across the floor. Gabby and Maddox were raring to get this day started. The siblings had heard the falls, seen the mist, yet still had not seen the falls with their own eyes. The pictures in the museum last night were amazing, and they could not wait to see them in person.

The kids' excitement level was sky-high as the family departed from the hotel. The Niagara scenic trolley rolled to a stop, and everyone climbed in.

"First stop, Cave of the Winds," a voice echoed from the loudspeakers as the trolley jumped forward and rolled down the road. Gabby and Maddox were amazed at the wide array of flowers and trees that lined the path. To their right was a water fountain that changed colors, and to the left, they noticed pathways leading to the falls with a few vendors selling food and souvenirs. Mother and Father were both in awe of the size of the grounds and the falls as they came into view. The trolley came to a screeching halt, and several people unloaded.

"Are we getting off?" Maddox rose to his feet.

"Relax. We thought we would go to the overlook deck and see the falls before going to the Cave of the Winds.

Does that sound okay?" Father said. Gabby nodded, and Maddox eased back into his seat. The trolley lurched forward and, in a matter of moments, rolled to another stop.

"Observation deck."

Mother and Father stood as Gabby and Maddox leaped from the trolley car and darted down the wide sidewalk. Father grabbed Mother's hand and smiled as they jogged after the children.

The path opened up to a large deck that overlooked the massive waterfalls. Gabby and Maddox stood in silence with their mouths wide open, gawking at one of the wonders of the world.

The roar was deafening, and the mist hung in the air. Maddox pointed to a sign as he walked over. "About 600,000 gallons of water travel down the falls every second. That equates to 5.5 billion gallons per hour." Maddox and Father made eye contact. "Wow!" Maddox looked back to the sign and continued to read. "About twenty percent of the drinking water in the United States goes over Niagara Falls." Maddox looked at Father. "Does that mean the water we drink in Ohio comes from here?"

"That's a good possibility... I guess it could." Father smiled.

Gabby darted over with Mother at her side. "Did you know Niagara Falls is three waterfalls? The Horseshoe Falls," Gabby pointed at the large horseshoe-shaped falls before them, "Bridal Veil Falls," Her hand moved toward a smaller set of falls, "and the American Falls." Her hand moved to the falls next to the railing. "They also overlap Canada and the United States."

"I think that's what the sign said last night in the museum." Maddox stuck out his tongue.

"There's no need for that." Father stared at Maddox. "I think she's excited, as we all are."

"Sorry, Gabby." Maddox bounced on his toes. "This place is amazing!" He waved a hand in a circular motion to encompass everything around them.

Gabby's gaze darted back and forth on the sign. "No way, that's impossible." The two jumped up and down with excitement. "Fish travel over the falls, and about ninety percent of them survive. Experts believe that the white foam from the rushing waters cushions their fall," Gabby read out loud.

"I wonder if we would survive going over the falls?" Maddox blurted out.

"There will be no talk like that. No one is going over the falls on my watch." Mother crossed her arms.

Maddox jumped up into Father's arms to get a better look over the railing. "Are those people?" Maddox pointed to a deck near the base of the falls. "What are they doing down there?" Maddox questioned. "If it's dangerous, I want to go." Maddox leaped from Father's arms and bounced up and down like a ball on the playground.

"Me, too!" Gabby jumped beside her brother.

"Calm down." Mother waved her hands. "That's the Cave of the Winds, and yes, we are going to go there next."

"Yeah," Gabby and Maddox cheered in unison as they both chuckled and skipped down the sidewalk.

Father grabbed Mother's hand again. "We better keep up, dear." The two smiled and trotted after the children.

They watched as the trolley rolled to a stop. Gabby and Mother climbed up the stairs, while Father helped Maddox to his seat. The trolley rolled forward, and before they even had a chance to say, "are we there yet," the trolley came to a halt. They climbed down and watched as the tram pulled away. They walked down a narrow path, where they came to a small building with a sign posted out front: *Cave of the Winds. Enjoy an elevator ride 175 feet deep into the Niagara Gorge. Put on the bright yellow poncho with special footwear, and follow your guide on a series of wooden walkways to our famous "Hurricane Deck."*

The walkways and deck are removed every fall for safety and rebuilt in the spring before they open for the summer, the sign stated. "Interesting fact." Gabby pointed to Mother, who nodded.

They made their way inside, and Father strolled over to the counter to purchase tickets, while Gabby and Maddox browsed about the gift shop. Father walked up and motioned them to some benches located near the elevator. Once in their seats, Father passed each of them a bright yellow poncho, a plastic bag, and special Niagara Falls flip-flops to wear.

"Take off your shoes and socks, and place them in the bag," Father instructed. "Then I'll lock them in a locker." He pointed to the row of lockers mounted to the wall.

"Ah, Dad, can I hold the key?" Maddox smiled.

"It's going to be windy and wet; that's why they call it the Cave of Winds." Father tucked the keys into his pocket as Maddox frowned.

They joined several other families in front of the elevator as a tall, lanky man wearing a bright orange poncho walked to the front of the crowd. His bushy, gray beard covered his mouth as he spoke. "Welcome to the Cave of Winds. You are about to descend to the bottom of Niagara Falls. It's going to be windy and noisy when we get to the bottom, so please pay attention. You need to stay together and walk slowly as the deck is slippery. Your special flip-flops are designed to give you extra traction when walking on wooden walkways and decks. We will make our way from the cave to the walkways, and you will follow the path to the Hurricane Deck. Please stay to the right to give groups that are leaving the chance to get by you. Once we get to the main deck, you can go play in the water. Does anyone have any questions?" He glanced around the room. "Great!" He reached out and pushed the button, and the large elevator doors slid open.

The crowd pushed and shoved their way inside as the doors closed behind them. Gabby tugged on Mother's arm and grabbed her hand in delight. Maddox followed her lead and placed his hand on Father as he gazed upward and smiled. The elevator plunged downward at a steady pace before coming to a stop. The doors opened, and a cool breeze slapped them in the face. They made their way out into the large, circular cave that opened before them. The crowd slowly cleared, and Gabby and Maddox could see the long, narrow tunnel ahead. The second set of elevator doors opened, and out marched another group of people. A small girl smiled and made her way over to Gabby. "Hi, do you remember me?" Addie asked in a soft voice.

"Hi guys." Maddox spun around to greet Knox and his brother Zander.

"What did you think of the ride down here?" Knox asked.

"I thought it would be longer, but I guess the elevator dropped quickly," Maddox replied.

"It looks like our kids have made new friends," the woman said, then introduced herself and her husband to Mother and Father. The two families merged and slowly made their way into the tunnel. A row of lights dotted the walls, and they began to make their way to the light at the end.

Thousands of seagulls squawked and buzzed back and forth as the group cleared the tunnel entrance. Maddox tugged his hood up, and just in the nick of time, as bird droppings hit the top of his poncho. Knox and Zander laughed and pointed when a few more bird droppings landed on Zander's arm. "It's dangerous out here." Father laughed as he and Mother both pulled their hoods over their heads.

Maddox gazed down the path toward the bottom of the falls. With each step, the roar grew louder. The five kids paused and looked over the deck. The rushing water loomed above, dousing each of them with a generous spray as they made their way up to the Hurricane Deck. Father stood back and snapped a few pictures with his phone. The thundering roar made it impossible to talk as Mother and Father just watched the kids stomp, splash, and dance around in the spray.

"Let's play tag," Knox hollered.

"Tag, you're it." Maddox tagged Gabby as he darted to the far side of the railing.

"No, you didn't!" she yelled and gave chase before changing directions and running after Knox.

Knox weaved and danced, trying to avoid Gabby, but she was quicker than he thought, and she slapped his left arm. "Tag, you're it!" she screamed and laughed.

It quickly became a game of two as Maddox, Addie, and Zander watched Gabby and Knox play touch. Maddox frowned and had a great idea. "Hey, do you two want to play tag?" He pointed to Addie and Zander.

"Sure." Addie giggled and ran in circles, trying to avoid Maddox's hands. Zander followed his sister's lead and darted about in large circles. Maddox could have touched them time after time, but he was too busy having fun to care about Gabby and her new boyfriend.

Mother tucked her arm around Father as he caught a glimpse of a smile from under her hood.

The other parents did the same, taking pictures and enjoying the sights. Minutes passed, quickly turning into

an hour. The siblings were exhausted and soaked to the core. The ponchos had given way to the force of the falls, and Gabby and Maddox stood before their parents in soggy clothes.

"I think it's time we had some lunch and let you guys dry out a little." Father laughed and smiled at the pair. The two families joined forces—after all, why break up such a precious moment? Gabby and Knox led the way back to the tunnel. Little Addie grabbed Knox's hand as Zander grabbed his other, while Knox looked at each of them, and his smile grew wide.

"I think your son is going to grow up to be a great dad."

"I would agree with you." The two men smiled as they watched Maddox and the two younger kids swing their arms and skip down the path.

"You have a lovely family," Mother mentioned to her new friend.

"I think you have a great family as well." The two women smiled as they strolled down the tunnel. The large group crammed into the elevator when the doors opened. After the short ride in the elevator, they found themselves back in the gift shop, where each child was allowed to pick out one souvenir.

Maddox darted toward the locker. Father unlocked it and handed out the dry towels they were given. After drying off, Maddox slipped on his dry socks and shoes, and Gabby quickly slipped outside to enjoy the heat of the sun. Someone tugged at her sleeve, and as she looked downward, she noticed Addie gazing up at her. "That was fun." Gabby smiled, and the little girl beamed and giggled.

Maddox stood next to Gabby, and Knox and Zander quickly joined the group. "Listen up, everyone. We've decided to have lunch together," Father said as he pointed at the diner next to the gift shop. The kids erupted in cheers.

"I hope they have cheeseburgers," Knox blurted out.

"I like cheeseburgers too, but only with ketchup," Gabby added with a shy grin.

Maddox frowned and thought she was being silly over a boy. He turned his attention to Addie and Zander, who were loving every minute of it. The two families enjoyed lunch and had a nice chance to dry out before their next adventure…

But what would that be?

Seven

The Maid of the Mist

Hours slipped away, and it was getting late in the day. The adults decided they had enough time to tackle one more adventure before dinner. After a brief debate, they decided on the Maid of the Mist. The boat ride would take them upriver, past the American and Bridal Veil Falls, and stop at the base of the Horseshoe Falls, the largest of the three falls.

The children hopped, skipped, and jumped down the sidewalk, making their way to the Maid of the Mist gift shop. Upon arrival, the two moms ushered the kids to the waiting area and the dads collected the tickets and blue ponchos they would be allowed to keep as souvenirs.

"So…" Knox paused, trying to make conversation, "what do you like to do, Gabby?"

"Um, I take dance class…" She gave a half smile.

"Do you not like dance?"

"I do, but I would prefer to play baseball like my brother."

"That's cool. I like baseball, but I love hockey. I skate and play on a junior league team. We're not that good, but we try to have a lot of fun playing. We won two games this season." Knox beamed with pride.

"Hockey is too rough for girls, but I think my dad watches it a little," Gabby said.

"Hockey is for everyone." Knox looked puzzled. "Why don't you play baseball?"

"Well, my mom loves to watch me dance, and I don't want to disappoint her."

"Can't you do both?"

"Interesting. I never thought about that." Gabby stared at the ceiling, trying to reason with herself about how that would work. "Sometimes I dance at the same time my brother has a ball game. I don't think that would work." Gabby frowned.

"Then you have to tell your mom how you feel. Just be honest with her. You like to dance but would love to try out for baseball. It seems like a quick fix, if you ask me." Knox made eye contact with Gabby.

"Well," Gabby's face grew red as she looked away to avoid eye contact. "Sure, I mean… why not? What do I have to lose, right? I'll let my mom know the minute we get back home. Thank you." Gabby gave Knox an awkward pat on the arm.

Maddox jumped up and down as Father handed him a poncho. "This is gonna be so cool," he blurted out. Knox turned to him and agreed. They slowly pushed forward toward the elevator, where they would descend to the bottom of the gorge. Once everyone had gathered, both families entered the elevator, and it began to move.

The doors slid open, and the bright sunlight blinded them for a moment. Gabby lowered her head to let her eyes adjust, and she noticed little Addie was doing the same. Gabby put her right foot out, and so did Addie; Gabby then placed her left foot forward and was not surprised when Addie did the same. Gabby started dancing, and Addie quickly joined in.

"Alright you two, calm down," Mother mentioned. "There are too many people gathered in line, and we need to be respectful of others." The two girls smiled and giggled as they stopped dancing.

Maddox's eyes grew as the large electric boat pulled into the dock. Once the vessel was unloaded, the line pushed and shoved forward. Both mothers helped and ensured that each child was safely on board as they all made their way to the upper deck, where they would have a great view of the falls.

"Welcome aboard the Maid of the Mist," the captain announced over the intercom. "We are about to embark on a journey to the base of the Horseshoe Falls, where 600,000 gallons of water flow over every second."

"Wow," Maddox interrupted. "That's a lot of cups of water."

Father squeezed Maddox's hand and whispered, "Pay attention."

"In 1846, the first Maid of the Mist—which was a steam-powered engine—was launched. This new boat is all electric and will power up the river." The captain paused. "I will have to run at full power to make it to the base of the falls since the force of the water will be pushing us backward. So please, hold on tight and remember to stay behind the railing at all times, or I will have to turn the boat around. Let's have a safe trip," the captain finished.

The horn blared, and everyone covered their ears. "I didn't expect that," Knox told Maddox.

"Me either." He smiled, then turned his attention to the front as the boat slowly pulled away from the dock. The large vessel drifted toward the middle of the river.

"We are just going sideways," Gabby mentioned, and Knox nodded as the electric engine roared to life.

The boat pushed forward at a slow pace. Then, the captain shifted to second gear and the speed increased. Gabby, Maddox, and Knox swayed back and forth, trying to find their footing. The boat slowed as they came in line with the American and Bridal Veil Falls.

"I didn't realize there were so many rocks at the base of the falls." Gabby pointed.

"They are more like boulders, if you ask me," Knox commented.

"I don't think I asked you," Gabby snipped and quickly realized she was not talking to her brother.

"I guess she told you." Maddox smiled and laughed at Knox.

"I think you are correct." Knox grinned and put a little distance between Gabby and him.

"I'm sorry… that sounded harsh. I didn't mean it like that." Gabby frowned.

"It's all good." Knox laughed and turned to look at the falls as the boat sped up and made its way past the American Falls, toward the massive half-circle-shaped falls that lay before them. The boat bobbed and swayed as they continued their journey.

The wind increased, and a fine mist sprayed their faces as birds buzzed back and forth. Everyone raised their hoods to cover their hair and tried to stay as dry as possible. Mother reached down and pulled two plastic straps and tied them in a small knot around Maddox's chin. "Mom, I can do this myself," he whined and pushed back.

Gabby smiled and giggled. "Momma's boy."

Knox chuckled and stepped forward, placing one foot on the bottom rail. He pushed up and moved his arms out to his sides. "Look at me, I'm flying."

"This isn't the Titanic, silly," Gabby said.

"Knox! Get down from there!" Knox's father yelled.

"Yes, Dad." Knox placed his feet back on the deck floor. The full sight of the falls came into view. The spray from the water slapped them in the face as the thunderous roar of the water pounded the river below. Seagulls and other birds squawked above. From time to time, one bird would swoop into the river to catch a fish that didn't survive going over the falls.

The engine screamed, trying to push forward. The force of the water pushed them back and held them at a safe distance. Trying to get a better view of the falls, Maddox wiped the water from his eyes. He had never seen anything this large before, as the base stretched over several football fields in length. The boat struggled to move forward and just drifted from side to side, giving them plenty of time to take in the scene. The boat slowly turned, giving them a view from one side of the falls to the other.

The hum of the engine slowed as the boat began to drift backward. Then, a horn rang out as the boat slowly turned around. Maddox danced from side to side and had an odd look on his face.

"What are you doing?" Gabby asked.

"Nothing…" He gave her a sidelong look from under the hood of his poncho.

"Don't give me that." Gabby smirked. "I can tell something is wrong."

"Okay… I have to go to the bathroom." He danced a little more.

Gabby laughed and smiled as she tapped Knox on the shoulder. Knox turned to see Maddox dancing. "Whatcha doing, man?"

"He has to pee," Gabby whispered just out of earshot of her parents.

Knox nodded, then poked Maddox and gave him an evil grin. "In Canada, we always say, 'Never pass up an opportunity to use a restroom.' You should have gone back at the gift shop." He danced a little, throwing his arms outward.

"I didn't have to go then; besides, it's the sound of the water that caused this." Maddox pranced about uncomfortably.

"The Horseshoe Falls was amazing. Did you like them?" Gabby asked Addie and Zander. Addie nodded yes, while Zander's smile told Gabby everything she needed to know. The unique shape and the amount of water that flowed over them were stunning. No wonder they were considered one of the eighth wonders of the world.

The wind and water spray lessened as the boat drifted to the left side of the river to make room for another boat to venture up to the falls. "Ladies, gentlemen, boys, and girls. We are now on the Canadian side of the river. If you have never been to Canada… well, you are now, eh." The captain's voice echoed out of the speakers.

"So, I can tell people I've been to Canada?" Maddox tugged on his father's poncho.

"Well, technically, yes…" Father hesitated. "But only on water, so you can't say you stepped foot in Canada. Does that make sense?"

"Yes." Maddox frowned as the boat slowed and pulled into the dock. One by one, they walked up the gangway toward the sidewalk that led to the elevator. After a quick ride up, they found themselves in yet another gift shop. Maddox darted to the bathroom, leaving Mother and Father a bit puzzled. "Is your brother alright?" Father asked Gabby.

"He'll be fine … as long as he made it in time." A sly smile covered Gabby's face.

Father shook his head and took off his poncho, tucking it into the plastic bag. Then he collected Mother, Gabby, and Maddox's ponchos as he appeared from the bathroom. "Do you feel better?" Father asked with a smile.

"Yes." Maddox laughed. "Can we buy something?"

"You have a one-track mind, son." Father paused, taking in his children's "please" faces. "Fine, one item each." The siblings darted about the store until each of them showed up with one special item. Maddox had grabbed a small metal boat that looked exactly like the boat they had just ridden, while Gabby wanted a calendar to hang on her wall with plenty of pictures of the falls.

"I'm hungry," Knox hollered to his father as they stepped outside.

Both dads looked at their watches. "Dang, it's dinner-time already."

"Would you and your family like to join us for dinner?" Father asked.

"Oh, I wish we could, but we already have plans to meet up with some of our friends. You know," he paused, "you're all welcome to join us if you like."

"Thank you for the offer, but we wouldn't want to impose. Besides, I promised the kids we would eat and then watch the colored lights reflect on the water after the sun goes down."

"It was nice to meet you, and I look forward to seeing you all soon." The guys shook hands, and the women hugged. Addie, Zander, and Knox said their goodbyes and waved as they slowly walked away.

Maddox and Gabby both waved as a touch of sadness came over them.

Eight

The Helicopter Ride

Morning brought a new day and more adventures. Today would be a helicopter ride over the falls and, of course, plenty of pictures. Thank goodness for the digital age of photography. When Mother and Father were growing up as kids, they had to have their film developed, which was expensive. In the digital world, people could take as many pictures as they like, and if they didn't like one, they could delete it. Plus, they get to see the picture the second they snap the camera. My, how times have changed… Mother was excited for the opportunity to take lots of pictures—of the scenery, but most of all, pictures of her family, both posed and candid—since it was her hobby.

They hustled about and made their way over to the helicopter pad. There was a long line, but thanks to Father, who purchased the tickets the day before, the family was on the second flight of the day. The children watched the first flight lift off, and the sound of the blades whirling about made them put their hands over their ears.

A tall, lanky man approached, carrying a box of bright orange earmuffs. They didn't look fluffy like the ones Gabby would wear when it was cold outside; these were solid and designed to stop the noise. "Hi folks, it's just the four of you, correct?"

"Yes." Father smiled and grabbed a small set from the box and placed it over Maddox's head. Then Father handed Gabby a set. "Do you need help? Or are you my big girl today?"

"Dad, I'll be ten soon, so no, I don't need help like my baby brother." Gabby smirked.

"Excuse me, I'm not a baby!" Maddox yelled as he looked upward and yelled again, "I'm not a baby!"

"You don't have to yell; we can hear you." Father pulled one side of the ear cover over so Maddox could hear. Maddox forced a smile as he realized he couldn't hear because of the earmuffs.

Gabby sneered at Maddox and quickly stuck out her tongue when Mother and Father were not looking. Maddox wrinkled his nose and stuck out his tongue at Gabby. Then the two of them smiled when Father tapped them on the shoulders and pointed toward the stairs. They watched as the helicopter began its descent and gently touched down in the landing zone. The blade that circled above slowed and finally came to a stop. One of the crew members darted out on the landing pad and placed a small stepstool by the door. Then, he reached up and lowered the handle, and the door popped open. He reached out his hand and helped a small girl out of the helicopter. She was followed by a taller girl, and Gabby guessed they were sisters. *Wow, what would it be like to have a sister instead of a brother?* Then a woman and a taller fellow quickly stepped out.

The man motioned for them to come over and instructed Gabby to step up first. This allowed Gabby a window seat on the right side. Father sat in the middle, and Maddox sat on the left window side. Mother had taken the front, where she would be able to sit in the passenger seat, giving her a front and side view—perfect for the scenic pictures she was excited to take. The attendant made sure he buckled them all in and gave an extra tug to double-check his work. He closed the door and backed away, then gave the pilot a thumbs up.

Gabby and Maddox's mouths hung open as the helicopter lifted upward. A weird feeling pulled at their tummies as the craft lifted straight up. The large river appeared below as Gabby and Maddox planted their faces against the glass. Father looked over Maddox's shoulder to catch a glimpse. The river grew wider as the chopper went higher in the sky. They were moving upriver from the falls and about a thousand feet or so in the air as the pilot began moving toward Horseshoe Falls. He slowly circled over the Canadian side, then went back and forth, giving everyone an excellent view. He motioned with his hands, pointing at all the birds—mainly seagulls—circling the water near the bottom of the falls, looking for fish that didn't survive the plunge. There must have been ten thousand birds; they were easy to see from this view.

The chopper moved toward the American Falls and Bridal Falls. The pilot pointed at the Maid of the Mist pulling away from the dock, and then to the lower wooden walkways at the base of the falls, called the Cave of Winds—two activities the family had already enjoyed. They then went downriver, and the chopper hovered over the gorge. Gabby and Maddox noticed the large rapids ahead, which had not been seen before since it was downstream. The helicopter circled again, giving everyone a great view of the large rapids before making his way back upriver toward the falls. He circled one more time, giving Mother plenty of time to snap her pictures before heading back to the landing zone.

The chopper lowered and gently touched down as the blades on top stopped rotating. The doors swung open, and Gabby, Maddox, Mother, and Father were told to step in front of the helicopter for a photo-op. Mother squealed with the opportunity for a family photo as she handed the man her camera. Father wrapped his arms around the kids, and Mother snuggled in close as the man took several photos. Father smiled, knowing Mother was happy.

The family exited the landing area before going into the gift shop, where they turned in the earmuffs. "Ah, now I can hear again." Maddox stretched his mouth and pulled on his ears.

"It's not like we were in an airplane." Gabby sneered. "I'm sure your ears don't hurt, so you don't need to pop them," Gabby corrected him.

"It's okay; leave your brother alone." Father patted Gabby's shoulder as he stretched his mouth and pulled on his ears.

Maddox wrinkled his nose and sneered back at Gabby. "Oh, can I buy this helicopter?" Maddox squealed, picking one up from the gift shop shelf.

"That looks rather expensive," Mother whispered, and motioned for Maddox to put it back. "Maybe something a little smaller, okay, dear?"

Gabby found a small glass paperweight labeled Horseshoe Falls with a tiny helicopter inside, while Maddox picked up a new toy helicopter. "Look, Mom, the blades spin!" Maddox said as he gave them a push and watched them rotate. Father pulled out his wallet to pay for the items before they made their way outside, where things were a little quieter.

"Look, it's a walking path." Maddox pointed. "Can we go, Mom? Can we?" Maddox pleaded, bouncing on his feet.

"Sure, why not? I enjoy walks through nature." Mother smiled as she grabbed Father's hand, and the four of them went upriver on the trail to explore.

Bees buzzed about, birds chirped in the trees, and the roar of the river faded the farther they walked from the falls. They came to a small clearing where the path forked — one continued upriver while the other led to a narrow bridge and a little island. Maddox tugged on Father's arm in the direction of the island. Mother nodded, and the four of them went single file over the wooden plank bridge. There were several benches where you could sit to enjoy the view of the river. "It's so wide I can barely see the other side," Maddox pointed.

Several large rocks stuck out of the water as the water swirled around them. Gabby stood on a small dock and leaned over to see if she could spot any fish. "Don't swim downstream," Gabby instructed the fish. "I don't want you to die."

"Over here," Maddox hollered as he pointed to another small path and a sign that read, *Ideal picture location ahead*. Mother and Father held hands and followed the kids down the path. A small shack came into view, where a small walkway led to a large barrel bobbing in the water.

Nine

The Barrel Ride

"Howdy folks." A short, stout man appeared. "Only five bucks for a picture of the kids in the barrel." Oh, Mother was hooked the moment the man said picture.

"I can photo shop the image and insert them going over the falls," Mother said as the man nodded.

"Is it safe?" Father asked, pointing to the barrel sitting in the water.

"Of course, it's safe. I have two ropes secured to the top and a chain with an anchor fastened to the bottom." He pointed to each of the ropes and at the water, where a chain floated.

"Please, please, Father!" Gabby jumped up and down.

"Come on, Dad. This will be fun," Maddox begged while he puffed out his lip.

"How can I resist that face? Sure, why not?" Before the words were out of his mouth, the kids darted toward the barrel.

"Hold up a minute," the old man said, stopping the kids in their tracks. "Sir, that will be ten dollars."

"What? You said five."

"Five dollars *each*."

"Oh, give him ten, dear. This will make a great picture and an awesome addition to our wall of memories," Mother persuaded with a twinkle in her eye.

Father pulled out his wallet and handed over ten dollars with a little bit of a frown. The old man smiled, then pulled out a little ramp and moved it over to the barrel. He extended his hand first to Gabby and helped her up the ramp and into the barrel. "There you go, little lady." Gabby looked shocked as the container bobbed up and down in the water.

Maddox ignored the old man's hand and darted up the ramp and jumped into the wooden drum, sending waves outward. Maddox turned and tipped his hat to Mother as she snapped a few photos. "Hey, what's this for?" Maddox held up a rope connected to the barrel.

"Put that down, sonny," the old man roared.

"Okay." Maddox shrugged and dropped the rope over the side. The cylinder shifted and pulled a foot or two from the dock.

"Pull them back!" Father yelled and lunged for the other rope just as it snapped past his fingertips. The barrel bobbed up and down a bit as it drifted outward into the river.

"What have you done?" Gabby squealed, a raspy sound in her voice.

"I didn't do anything; I only touched the rope."

"Exactly!" Gabby yelled as she looked back to see the panic in Mother and Father's eyes.

"What about the anchor?" Father howled.

"Well… I don't have one, exactly—" the old man confessed.

"Are you kidding me?" Father shook his head. "Give me a rope; I'll toss it to them," Father snapped, his tone harsh.

"I don't have one; I'm sorry," the old man pleaded.

"Call 911," Mother yelled.

The old man darted a few feet away and picked up his black backpack. Pulling out his phone, he called for help.

The barrel drifted farther from shore, spinning slightly from the current of the upcoming rapids. Mother and Father darted back over the little island to the path and followed along the shoreline. Father motioned for them to paddle back. A few times, Father jumped in the water but realized the force of the water was too strong, and he would not be able to help his children if he got swept up in the rapids.

Gabby extended her arm over the side, and Maddox did the same. Gabby's arm barely touched the water, and Maddox's didn't even reach the water. Gabby looked to the bottom of the barrel and grabbed a small step stool and extended it over the side. She then scooped it into the water, using it as an oar.

"We're not making any progress," she yelled at Maddox. "We're heading toward the falls!" A tear traced down her cheek.

"We're going to be fine." Maddox pointed to a helicopter circling above. "They will help us." He smiled. "I wonder if we are on the news?"

"That won't matter if we go over the falls, silly! Sometimes you can be so..." Gabby stopped, clenched her fist, and jumped up and down, sending waves outward, "foolish."

"Everything's going to be fine." Maddox tried to comfort his sister. The water swirled, sending the barrel into a spin. They were now about fifty feet from the shore. Mother and Father paced the shoreline, watching helplessly as they begged for help from anyone who would listen.

Gabby cried louder, and Maddox hugged her. "It will be alright. Maybe we should jump out and swim for it?"

"You know I'm not that good of a swimmer, and neither are you."

"It's better than doing nothing," Maddox countered.

"I'll never even get the chance to play baseball," Gabby wailed as tears flooded her eyes.

"Look! A second helicopter!" Maddox pointed to the sky. "See, I told you they'd help!"

The side door opened, and a rope ladder dropped down, making its descent toward the children. The flow of the river picked up, and the helicopter was having a hard time matching their speed. The ladder was only a few feet over their heads, and Maddox jumped up but was unable to reach the ladder. Gabby lunged upward and touched the bottom rung with her fingertips. The barrel jerked forward and spun to the side when they crashed into a large rock that stuck out of the water.

Gabby and Maddox buckled over and tried to regain their legs. The up-and-down motion was making Maddox sick. "I think I'm going to throw up…"

"You're fine." Gabby stared and nodded, and Maddox returned the nod. "We need to get it together." Maddox signaled his agreement. The mist hung heavy in the air as the ladder chased after the barrel, though it seemed to stay a few feet behind.

"When we get out of this, I'm trying out for baseball, and I'm going to knock the ball out of the park on my first at-bat." Gabby's stern voice was all Maddox needed to hear.

"Let me get on your shoulders. Then I can reach the ladder, and we can get out of this mess." Gabby smiled, liking his plan. She bent over, allowing Maddox to get on her shoulders. She slowly stood as the ladder appeared over them, and Maddox latched on to the bottom rung.

"I got it," he cheered. A brief smile crossed Gabby's face, knowing he would be safe. But how was she going to get out of this mess her brother had created? Maddox crashed down on top of Gabby.

"Sorry, I couldn't hang on; it's too slippery."

"Take this stool," Gabby said, her voice forceful. "Lean over the side and row with everything you got. I'll hold your feet. I promise I won't let go."

Maddox took the stool and leaned over the edge, and Gabby latched on to his feet, bracing her feet against the front of the barrel. Maddox dipped the stool into the water and began to row. It was working; they were slowly making their way toward the shore. The real question was, did they have enough time to make it, or would they go over the falls?

"I love you," Gabby squealed in delight as they inched closer to the trees. The water's speed increased and swirled, making the journey almost impossible.

"I love you, too," Maddox echoed back.

Maddox's arms grew tired and burned with every stroke. He knew this was all his fault, and he was determined to get them out of this mess. He remembered when they had met Spark, a little trumpet-sounding alien who had helped them find their way home when they were lost in space.

"Spark, can you hear me? Because if you can, we sure do need you," he whispered. He remembered he didn't have the little stone to rub, so he doubted Spark would arrive in time. He stroked the water with force and tried to think positive. *I can do anything I set my mind to. I got this.* He dipped the stool into the water over and over and over again. He glanced up to see Mother and Father's smiling faces only a few feet away. Father extended his hand, but Maddox forced himself to keep rowing.

They were going to be alright after all.

Maddox's grew tired as a sharp pain pierced his arm. He slowed as he dropped the stool.

"Hey, daydreamer, wake up," Gabby chuckled and grabbed the old man's hand as he helped her out of the barrel. Gabby turned to face Maddox, "Why are you smiling?"

"Hey sonny, are you coming? I have other people waiting." The old man extended his hand. Maddox was a bit confused. He looked left, then right. They had never left the dock. He smiled and chuckled to himself as he took the old man's hand and got out of the barrel.

"What were you thinking about?" Father asked.

"I saved us," Maddox smiled and winked at his dad.

Father smiled back as the family walked back to the little island, sat on the benches, and looked at the wonderful pictures Mother had taken.

Later that afternoon, they met up with their new Canadian friends, had dinner, and said their goodbyes. Gabby and Knox exchanged emails and promised to keep in touch.

Ten

The BirthDay Party

Another adventure had come to a close. The trip to Niagara Falls had been awesome. Mother was happy, especially since she had a ton of new pictures of Gabby and Maddox she could post online—along with all of her fond memories. She even stayed in touch with their new Canadian friends, thanks to email and social media.

The car coasted to a halt. Gabby and Maddox flung the doors open and raced to the front door. "Hold up, guys." Father walked up as he pulled the house keys from his pocket and tossed them to Gabby.

"Great catch, sis."

Boots and Momma sprang to attention when they heard the keys in the lock and bounced about with joy. Someone was here, and they hoped it would be Gabby and Maddox. The lock clicked, the door popped open a little, and the familiar footsteps of the kids made Boots and Momma prance in circles.

"Boots, Momma!" Maddox and Gabby said in unison. Mother and Father smiled from the doorway as Gabby and Maddox each picked up a cat to hug dearly. After a few moments, they swapped cats. Momma and Boots were on top of the world.

Two weeks slipped past, and the weekend had arrived. This day was not just a regular Saturday; it was a special Saturday. Mother and Father hustled about, prepping things for the big event, while Gabby and Maddox sat outside on the swing set, so they would not get in the way. Soon, families began to arrive, some staying, others dropping off a child or two. When the house was full of friends and family, Mother called Gabby and Maddox inside to join them.

"Happy Birthday, Gabby," the crowd cheered and yelled when Gabby made her entrance. A large sign hung over the kitchen table that read *"Ten."* Nestled next to all the presents was a large sheet cake that remained covered. The siblings played with their friends from school and ate pizza until they couldn't eat anymore.

Mother uncovered the cake, and in the center was a giant ten surrounded by pretty girls dancing in colorful outfits. Gabby smiled and gave Mother and Father a hug. While Gabby figured she was about to get more dance outfits and shoes, she hid her pain because she didn't want to disappoint her mother.

It was finally time to open the gifts. One by one, Gabby opened each present. She was thrilled to receive so many new books, and her mind drifted to all the new places she would explore when she read them. Her next gift was a journal, and she was excited that she could record everything she did each day. She even received some new clothes that she wanted.

The big moment had arrived. What had Mother and Father gotten her, and what had Maddox done for his sister? She was sure Maddox had gotten her something stupid like last year, a silly candle. *What do I need a candle for? I'm too young to be playing with fire, Mother had said.* Gabby smiled and picked up the gift from Maddox.

"Wait, wait!" Maddox yelled. "Open mine last, please." Gabby hesitated, then laid the package back on the table. She picked up a mid-sized box. *Love Mother and Father*, the tag read. Gabby beamed and wondered what they could have come up with this year. She hadn't asked for much, though she was sure they wouldn't get her the laptop she requested—after all, she was only ten.

The box was light as she shook it to the left, then to the right, and up and down. Nothing rattled inside. Puzzled, she began to rip and tear the wrapping paper off. It was a plain shoe box, one of Father's. *What? My feet are not that big*, she thought to herself. Gently, she pulled the top off to find a bunch of white tissue paper hiding something beneath. Slowly, she pushed the paper to one side.

"No… way!" she screamed, pulling out a baseball glove and waving it for all to see. Some of the other girls frowned, but Gabby was on top of the world. The large, long box contained a shiny, pink aluminum Louisville slugger baseball bat. *Does this mean I am going to be able to play baseball? But how could they have known…?*

She whirled around the room in excitement, showing everyone her new glove and baseball bat.

"Gabby." Mother pointed to the table where one lonely box remained, Maddox's gift. Gabby waltzed over to the table, then slowly reached for the package. She gazed at Maddox, who had an evil grin on his face. Gabby nervously picked up the box, which was light as a feather. She shook the gift, and nothing moved inside. *Did Maddox prank me with an empty box?* She pulled the sloppy gift wrapping off. *When was he going to learn how to wrap a birthday gift properly?* She forgave him since he was only eight. She hesitated and stared at the brown box in her hand. One piece of tape held the box closed. *Here goes nothing*, she thought.

Gabby exhaled and removed the piece of tape, and the lid sprang open. Her eyes grew and bugged out of her head. She glanced at her brother, who was smiling, and then back at the box. Tears traced her cheek when she read the handwritten note from her brother.

"Welcome to the team!"

Gabby hoisted the baseball cap with the team logo into the air and beamed with pride. "I'm really on the team?"

"Yes." Several boys stepped forward, wearing the identical hat, patting her on the back and welcoming Gabby to the team.

"Now stop crying; you're embarrassing me," Maddox whispered in her ear.

Gabby embraced her brother tight and whispered back, "Thank you! How did Mom and Dad know?"

"I told them, and now everyone is happy." Maddox smiled as he embraced his sister. Mother and Father joined in the hug while Boots and Momma went back and forth, rubbing the family's ankles and legs to show their love and support.

"Here's to the best birthday ever!" Gabby screamed.

Book Club Questions

1. What did you enjoy about this book?

2. What are some of the major themes of this book?

3. Who was your favorite character? What did you appreciate about him/her?

4. Are you satisfied with the ending? Why or why not?

5. Did you find this book to be a quick read? Why or why not?

6. What scene do you remember best? Why do you think that is?

7. Describe your favorite part of the book.

8. Was there anything in the book that surprised you?

9. If you could be a character in the book for one day, who would you choose to be? Why?

10. If one of the characters could come to your house for dinner, who would you like to have visit?

11. If you had to pick one color to describe the book, what color would you pick? Why?

12. If you had to describe this book in one word, what word would you choose?

13. Were you satisfied with the ending of the story? Why?

14. Were there any new words that you learned from reading the book?

15. If you could ask the author one question, what would you ask?

16. What questions do you have after reading the book?

17. Do you have a friend who you think would like this book? Who is it? Why?

18. Does this author have any other books? Have you read any of them?

Acknowledgments

I'm a writer, so I mostly work alone. I greatly appreciate my wife Toni for putting up with my weird ways and allowing me the time I needed to complete this story.

Thank you to my daughter Jessica for working with me on this project. I valued all your suggestions, ideas, and criticism throughout the writing process.

Thank you to Silvia Curry, Phoenix Whirl, and Melissa Derr for finding those elusive mistakes that drive readers nuts. And thank you for all your thoughts and suggestions during the proofreading process.

Thank you to all the Alpha readers. Thank you to Carolyn Hornick and Teresa Thompson for taking time out of your day to read my story and tell me what worked and what didn't.

Thank you to Victoria Deutsch for your outstanding sketches. A special thank you to Vanity Diaz for adding the color and bringing the sketches to life.

A special thank you to all the children who read the Gabby and Maddox Adventure Series.

Author Bio

Steve Altier is an award-winning mystery, suspense author. He was born in a small town in central Pennsylvania (aka "Lizardville") where he grew up in the old dam keeper's house.

He now resides in Tampa with his wife Toni. Steve has four loving daughters and four cats.

He enjoys writing, reading, bowling, and spending time at amusement parks. He loves to travel, take trips to the beach, or lie around the pool with family and friends.

Learn more about Steve and his stories by following on social media or visit his website. www.stevealtier.com

Steve would love to hear from you. You can email him at stevealtierbooks@outlook.com